This is a work of fiction. Names, characters, places, and incidents either are the product of the author's imagination or are used fictitiously. Any resemblance to actual persons, living or dead, events, or locales are entirely coincidental

Cover and interior design by: TS Design Studio

Edited by: Jacqueline Chappell

Gina Davis

Tamera Fair

www. Somewomenpreferhell.com

DEDICATION

This book is dedicated to the women who choose to play with fire knowing they will get burned, women who choose excitement over safety. The women who choose to make their own decisions right or wrong and stand on them. The women who want the people closest to them to love them through it all.

I want you to know, you are not alone.

PART ONE

I would strongly suggest you pop a bottle of champagne and pour a tall glass. The shit I'm about to tell you is real and uncensored. I need you seated, with a group of friends.

Enjoy,

Modi

CHAPTER 1:

A SMILE

We had an amazing day, my sister, my mom and me. We went on a tour around Chicago first by bus, then by boat and we finished the day with dinner on the 95th floor in the John Hancock building. “Let me see your new condo," my sister said to my mom. Immediately I lit up like a Christmas tree. My eyes looked like I had just received a brand new Mercedes Benz. I stood up and I said, "Yes let's go." I'm in love with our new condo. We moved to this condo after a very intense argument between my mom and her boyfriend, Mike. The incident was traumatizing, I was 13 going on 14 and my sister was 16 going on 17. My mom had just gotten into a new relationship after being divorced from my father for eight years, with a man I like to call “the devil.” He was 6'7” about 300 pounds and very muscular. He went to the gym faithfully, like he was training to kill someone. His smile was conniving, like he had a hidden agenda.

The way he walked was very mysterious and sneaky. For a man that's about 300 pounds you would think his steps would make an earthquake. He had hands that could cover my entire face. My mom loved this huge hulk - like man. They did everything together until one summer.

At the start of this summer, he and my mom had been together for a year straight, no breaks. I would often wonder if she ever got tired of being suffocated by his big ass. I hated him from the moment I met him because he wasn't our father. This particular summer I grew to despise him. He would walk in the house every morning at around 4:00 AM from hanging out all night with God knows who. On this particular night he fumbled in around 4:45 AM sloppy drunk, running into everything, waking up the entire house. They argued about everything from the dishes to the dog and the cars in the garage. Speaking of the cars in the garage, he brought home a new Bentley Coupe the week prior. My mother was livid! After spending two days out with no communication he finally came home and thought the car would make her forget he hadn't been there. That night, she let it go, this night I guess she had time. Why you steady sweating me, badgering me. You knew what you were getting into, ain't this what got you here? Ain't this keeping you here? So your daughters can stay in that fancy ass school. So you can keep buying Gucci, Chanel, cars and clothes," Mike slurred to my mom. "Shut up!" my mom interrupted. "In case you forgot, I paid the mortgage the last four months because yo' ass think popping bottles in the club, and buying cars to stunt in the hood is more important than securing the roof over your head." Mike was embarrassed at that point. His pride was hurt, so he started charging towards my mom, who is 5'2" and maybe 140 pounds soaking wet against his big ass. It was inevitable that my mom would lose that battle. So I hopped out of my bed, ran upstairs to where my mom and Mike were. I pushed open the door (because it was only cracked) and screamed, "Get away from my mom!"

When I tried to stop them from arguing, he pushed me on the ground. I remember being more shocked than physically hurt. My mom was shocked as well and yelled to my sister and me to start the car. I refused to leave my mother so I stayed behind the door to see the outcome of the argument. My mom raised her hand to swing and hit him for pushing me on the ground. He grabbed her hand and she began to cry. He pulled her by her hand until she was to her knees. Her cries went silent, unable to cry out due to the pain. He looked up at the door and saw me there watching him hurt her. I thought he would stop but he only smiled. His smile did not indicate that everything would be OK. It was more of a " shit is about to get real" kind of smile, a demonic smile. I remember feeling helpless as he started to talk at my mother while she was trying to rub her hand after he released it. "I'm only with you for your credit. Don't you know I could have anybody?" he said to her as he packed up her things. Mike was throwing her clothes, shoes, purses and perfumes into a 64 gallon trash bag. I remember watching his facial expressions as he was doing this and thinking to myself, he has no emotions.

While I was watching him belittle every aspect of my mother's life, I tried to put together a plan for the three of us to get out of the house. I remembered my phone was in my pajama pants pocket, so I pulled it out to call my dad or my cousin, or any man who could safely get us away from this demon. To my surprise, my sister snatched my phone. "Mike, she's trying to call for help!" The look on my mother's face was that of defeat. It was two against two but the odds were not in my and my mom's favor.

My mom looked at my sister in disbelief. She said, "I thought I asked you and your sister to start the car." My sister immediately started to cry and told my mom, "He is the best thing that has ever happened to us. If we leave now, we will live a completely different life. Just let it go." That seemed to be the remark that triggered the restoration of my mother's courage.

She slapped my sister and reminded her, "When I'm done, you're done." "Mike, you can have all this shit. I was fine without you." After she said that to Mike, she grabbed my hand and we both ran to the car leaving my sister in the house. By the time we got in the car it was around 8:30 AM. She told me she didn't want to talk and for me to go to sleep and that once I woke up, everything would be better. I trusted her so I did as I was told. Mike's house was in the suburbs of Chicago, an hour and a half from downtown Chicago. I slept the entire car ride until I heard my mother say, "We're here!"

I wiped the sleep from my eyes to see where "here" was. I looked out of the window to see a building that seemed to never end. The vibe I got from the building was so tantalizing that I asked my mom "Are we staying with one of your friends for a while?" She said, No, this is our new home." Puzzled and perplexed as to how that was even possible when we just left Mike's and was basically homeless, so I thought. My mom finally told me that she had been planning to leave him for months. She went out and found a place for the three of us to live. I knew you weren't that naive, I thought to myself. We parked our car and went upstairs to our new condo, without my sister. The condo had three bedrooms, four bathrooms, and a view of Lake Michigan. It was fully furnished with clothes of my size and my sister's size in each bedroom. When I finally opened my mouth I said, "This is heaven." My mom smiled and went into her room and went to sleep.

Two months passed before my mom would answer the phone to speak to my sister. My mom wanted nothing to do with Mike and my sister who was still living with him. My mom thought my sister would tell Mike information about where we lived or how we were doing. She was uncertain of what information could be disclosed but she knew she wanted Mike to know nothing. The two months prior to my sister calling were amazing. I had just graduated 8th grade from a private school downtown which was five minutes away from our new condo. All my friends were in that neighborhood. Life was like heaven during those two months. My mom and I spent so much time together.

My sister called my mom's cell phone one day and I overheard her crying, begging my mom to come back "home." I walked away knowing my mom would never go back to that house, I just knew it was nothing Kai could say to her to make her change her mind so I was uninterested in the rest of their conversation. I should have stayed to hear the outcome.

A week after that conversation I came home from school and Kai was sitting on the couch in the lobby of our condo building. She ran to me, picked me up, and said, "Oh my God Kana it's been two months and you've gotten bigger." I looked at Kai, unhappy to see her and asked her where my mom was. My mom came off the elevator and said “OK girls let’s go.” “What's going on ma, where are we going?” I asked in a very concerned voice I asked. “We are going to have a family day, just you me and your sister.” I was completely against it but I actually ended up enjoying the day, I couldn't wait for my sister to ask to see the condo. Once we got upstairs into our condo my mom showed Kai her room. Kai seemed unimpressed and walked out of the room without so much as a thank you. Kai then joined my mom and me in my mother’s room. “Are you ready?” Kai asked my mom. My mom looked at me and said, “Kana, go pack a bag, Mike wants us to come and talk to him.” So many emotions and questions came to me at once. Why would she even consider that? I knew Kai had something to do with it. Should I tell my father? What if we go back and he hurts her again? I was truly overwhelmed with negative thoughts, so I ran to my room, locked the door and screamed “I’m not going back there and it ain't shit you can do to make me." I forgot my mom had the key to my room door when I said that. She unlocked the door, grabbed me by my hair, dragged me down the hallway onto the elevator and then into the parking garage. She forced me to get in the car with her and Kai. I remember being in the back seat with tears falling down my face looking out of the window saying to myself, I pray I'm stronger than this when I get older.

"Shut up, before I give you something to cry about." I'm certain all Black mothers say this… but I digress. Eventually I cried myself to sleep. I woke up to Mike in the window with a Kool-Aid grin on his black- ass face. I wanted to tell my dad so bad, but unfortunately, my mother put the fear of God in me. Of course, I'm the last to get out of the car. My mom goes in first and hugs and kisses Mike for what seemed like an eternity. YUCK! I thought to myself. Kai has been living there the whole time so it wasn't a huge reunion for her and Mike. They do this "dap" thing with their fists when they see each other and it makes my stomach turn. I remember walking past him red puffy eyes and all. I said, “Hey Mike, How are you?” as I was looking down trying to avoid eye contact yet still be respectful. Who knows, my mother might have busted my lip for not speaking to her drug.

Mike made a feast for us: fried chicken (my favorite), cabbage, sweet potatoes, greens and sweet water cornbread. He was always a great cook and he knew that I would love this meal. It was really because of this meal that I was able to sit at the table with him and my family, and not seem as upset as I was. My mom knew how I felt about him so she pulled out the cards once we were done eating (by the way, dinner was silent). As soon as she pulled out the cards, Mike and Kai got excited. We used to play spades every Wednesday night when my mom and Mike first started dating a year ago. I remember feeling like, “Here she goes, trying to make a family with Satan again.” I played though because Kai and I are always partners and we always win. This particular day, Mike was trying to get my mom and me to move back in with him so he tried his hardest to make the game way more fun than it had ever been. He brought out a bottle of wine for him and my mom and Welch's sparkling grape juice (our favorite) for my sister and me to drink during the game. We played and laughed for a couple hours. In fact, I forgot where we were, what had already happened and that I hated him with a passion. I was reminded quickly when my mom followed him to what used to be their room as she told me that she and I would go to the community high school up the street where Kai was already going, to enroll me. We would be moving back into Mike's house.

I yelled, "Is it the fire you love? Or the fact that he's Satan himself that draws you into him." I was ignored by drunken laughs from both my mom and Mike. I thought about calling my father that night but I just went to sleep because clearly this is a battle for a professional, a 13- year-old didn't stand a chance.

CHAPTER 2:

SOMETHING'S UP

We moved back into Mike's house right before school started. It was my freshman year in high school and Kai's sophomore year. Over the summer, I turned 14 and Kai turned 17. The first week of school was interesting to say the least. "I'll be back in a week baby. I promise it'll go by quickly," my mom said to me as she was going out of the door. A week with Kai and Mike by myself! What if they've been plotting against me? It was always my mom and I against Mike and Kai. I once had no idea why Kai and Mike were so close, but then I found out. I certainly wish I still hadn't had any idea. Kai was beautiful. She's 5'1", 125 pounds, beautiful long black wavy hair, a very mature body, and a face like the late singer Aaliyah. To be honest, my sister "had it going on." When Kai took the phone from me when my mom and

Mike were fighting and I tried to call for help, I thought to myself, "something's up."

I didn't mention it to my mom because there was too much going on. I knew she would only want to focus on one thing at a time. This particular week I found out exactly what was up. My mom had to go to LA for a week on a business trip and I was left with Mike and Kai. For the first two days, the two of them wouldn't speak to me. They directed all of their questions to each other. When the food was ready, Mike would text Kai and tell her to come eat. I had to wait for the smell to reach me to know the food was ready. The fact that they didn't want to talk to me really didn't bother me at all. I was counting down the days until my mom would return. On Wednesday I'd had enough. I texted my mom to ask if I could stay at my friend London's house for the remainder of the week. My mom of course understood and without hesitation she replied, "Yes baby, I'll pick you up on my way in." London was my best friend whom I had met when I was five years old in ballet class.

London lived around the corner from Mike so she was already going to be attending the same community high school. London and I were the same age, but she had two older brothers that drove her everywhere she had to go. She and her two brothers came to get me from Mike's after school. "Kai, I'm leaving," I yelled upstairs. She ran down the 14 step staircase and gave me a hug and told me to be safe. I remember thinking, "Wow, that's the first thing she's said to me since my mom left. Should I stay and try to repair my relationship with my sister?" Immediately I told myself to walk out of the house when Mike began to walk down the stairs. "Does your mom know where you'll be Kana?" Mike asked me. I really wish I could have rolled my eyes and ignored him but my mom told me to always be respectful no matter how I feel inside. "Stay in a child's place" she would often remind me. "Yes, I texted her and asked if it would be okay to go to London's. She told me it was fine." When I told him what my mom said, his eyes were fixated on Kai. It got awkward so I left and got in the car with London. When we arrived at London's house, her mother told us to finish our homework and that by the time we were done, dinner would be ready. "Ms. Grant, I'm so sorry I left my backpack at Mike's house. I was in such a rush to leave I only grabbed my bag with my clothes." She assured me it wasn't a problem and that Larry, London's oldest brother would drive me back to get it.

I had a key to Mike's house so I opened the door, ran to my room which was on the first floor and grabbed my bag. I heard noises upstairs and it sound as though Kai was hurt. I dropped my bag and ran upstairs to where the sound was coming from. I went to Kai's room and it was empty. I went in the guest room and it was empty. I went into Kai's bathroom, empty. I really didn't think to go into Mike's room until I heard the sound again. The door was open but his room was all the way at the back of the hallway on the 2nd floor so unless one was to walk directly into the room, they wouldn't know what was going on. When I walked down the hallway the noises got louder, they began to sound foreign to me. Kai didn't sound hurt anymore. I was unfamiliar with the sound at the time. When I walked into the room, I saw bodies moving in the bed under the covers. I squinted my eyes to try to figure out what was going on, but my presence was made aware of and the two bodies came from under the covers, it was Kai and Mike. Immediately Kai started to explain, "Kana I promise it isn't what it looks like. Don't go telling mom something you're too young to comprehend." At that point, Mike was laughing. As though what I saw wasn't that bad. I ran downstairs as Kai was chasing me. I grabbed my backpack and ran out the door and got into the car with Larry.

"Drive off! Please don't stop to talk to my sister." That's what I told Larry and he did just that. Larry never liked Kai anyway.

London tells me all the time that Larry comes home talking about how Kai's attitude is so stank.

When we got back to their house, I was silent. I did my homework like I was told and ate my dinner. The Grants had a room set up for me, with fresh towels, brand new bed set and a set of pajamas. I went into the room, saw Ms. Grant and asked if it was okay to shut the door while I called my mother. She said that was fine and wished me a good night. I had twelve missed calls from Kai and six from Mike, I refused to talk to them because I, for one, had no idea what I had witnessed and two, because I knew exactly what I had witnessed. I texted my mom, "You need to come home ASAP." She called immediately and said "What's going on? Mike called and told me not to believe you because you didn't know what you saw. What did you see?" Crying, I said "I saw him in bed with Kai. They were under the covers with their bodies moving, making sounds. I'm 14 years old, but I know what I saw.

“I just don’t understand! “My mom yelled. She paused for a while. I could tell the news caught her off guard. Because I'm the baby, she never wants me to worry. She got it together quickly and assured me it was going to be OK. She wanted me to calm down. She said she would be on the next flight home. It was already 10:00PM, so I knew she meant in the morning. I texted her and told her to call Ms. Grant or London if she needed to speak with me because I was about to turn my phone off. That night I cried myself to sleep. I had no idea what was about to happen to my life or to my sister. I would always just “call” Mike the devil, but I had no idea my mom was really dancing with the devil.

"Kana, your sister is here to get you." Ms. Grant says to me through the door the next morning. I pretended to be sleep when she came to sit on the bed. “Kana wake up pretty," Ms. Grant says in her monotone, angelic voice as she softly pushed me in an attempt to wake me up. I opened my eyes because that's where

I draw the line. I hate being touched, even in a motherly way. I was still, absorbing last night's events. I hesitated to tell Ms. Grant that I wouldn't be getting up to go anywhere with my sister. I stretched for a couple of seconds to get my thoughts together. As I was letting out a yawn I said, "I'm going to sleep a little longer, and my mom will pick me up. Would you mind telling her that?" Before I could object, Ms. Grant yelled toward the kitchen, "Kai, we're back here." I thought to myself, I should have stayed asleep. When we were younger, my mom told my sister and me to keep family business within the family. Therefore, when Kai walked in, I forced a smile so Ms. Grant wouldn't know I hated her. "Hey Kai," I said very subtly. I could tell by the way she responded she was on edge and had no idea of my mood. "Morning Kana," she said with uncertainty. Kai sat on the bed and was about to begin to speak. Before she could, I interrupted and asked Ms. Grant if it would be OK for Kai and I to speak privately. Me asking for privacy in her house was a bit much, but she understood and exited the room gracefully. “Sure baby” she said and closed the door.

As soon as Ms. Grant shut the door, Kai said very fast and angrily, “I told you not to tell mom something you were too young to understand." I replied, very nonchalantly, “I told her what I saw." I could feel the tears forming behind my eyes, and so many thoughts filled my mind. For example, why did she get in bed with Mike and why does she continue to hurt my mother? I just let it go and asked her nothing. Kai began to cry softly at first, then profusely which was a shock to me. Kai never showed emotions. To her, everything was a joke until she was confronted with something she did wrong. Then she became a victim. I remained silent while Kai continued her very dramatic crying episode. There was some tissue on the nightstand that Kai pointed to, left of where my head was laying.

Might I add that I was lying on a very fluffy white goose down pillow that felt like heaven!

I didn't move when she pointed to the tissue. I pretended not to see her. “Kana don't be a bitch. Hand me a Kleenex." I wanted to throw the box at her and prayed that the squared end hit her in the eye. But instead, I pulled two pieces of tissue out of the box and handed them to her. I rolled my eyes so hard I swear I heard them pop.

Kai had no idea, that I dialed my mom’s cell number when she came into the room, so she could listen in on the entire conversation (pretty clever for someone too young to comprehend sex). Anyway, Kai continued her sob story going back and forth between, I lied to mom, and then Mike is to blame for manipulating Kai into bed with him. I barely spoke. She rarely gave me the opportunity to. The way she rambled made me think she was possessed or even worse, in love. She was so unsure of what story she wanted to be her truth. It was clear that Mike was to blame in this situation, and that Kai was delirious. Kai looked a bit more mature than she actually was.

My mom and dad adopted Kai as Mellani before I was born. After I was born, they changed her name to Kai to keep the K theme going. Kai was five when they adopted her but it was already too late to shield her from what she would become due to where she came from. Kai once overheard my mom say that she thinks Kai's birth mom's early influence will be the blame for the terrible decisions Kai is subject to make. Kai uses what she overheard to her advantage every chance she gets. As I continued to listen to Kai, I started to feel badly. What if she had no idea this was wrong? I thought to myself, and then I remembered a time when we were younger. Kai tried to play the victim and I fell for it. One day Kai told me I was adopted, I was seven years old and very impressionable. In fact, I'm certain all kids at that age are impressionable. Of course when she told me that, she was laughing. I probably did something to make her mad and that's why she said it.

"That's why you were adopted. The only reason you look like dad is because your real mother was dad's mistress, who was strung out on crack. Mom took you and raised you as her own." In my mind being told I was adopted was terrible but being told I was a crack baby was one of the darkest moments of my life. In those twelve minutes at age seven, I began to think that half of my life was a lie. I wanted answers of course. So, I ran upstairs to my mother's room. My eyes were red and puffy, snot was running down my nose, and I failed at every attempt to sniff it back up. My words were chopped because I hadn't finished crying. My mom said, "NaNa, what's the matter baby?" My parents gave me this nickname before I was born and to this day I still hate it with a passion. Moving on, my mom looked very concerned as to why I was so upset. She pulled me close and said, "NaNa baby, please tell me what's wrong. I hate seeing you so upset." The only thing I could get out at that moment was, "Kai said..." then came more cries and more failed attempts to sniff my snot back up. My mom yelled for Kai. "Kai Laila Steal, get your ass in here right now!" My mom would use our full names when we were in deep trouble. Kai came in about two minutes later, snarling at me, "You little brat!" My mom slapped her and said, "Do not laugh at your sister when she is upset. Now, what did you say that made her so sad?" Holding her face, Kai responded, "I told her she was adopted but I was just playing with her." My mom had a look on her face that you get when someone does something or says something to you but you have the upper hand and they don't know it- that look. "What did she tell you NaNa?" "She told me that dad had a mistress who was strung out on crack and that she was my birth mother. She said that you took me and raised me as your own." My mom started laughing nonstop. She looked at Kai, still laughing, and Kai looked back at her very angrily. My mom asked Kai," You want to tell her? Or should I?"

Kai ran downstairs and my mom said to me as her laugh lightened, "Baby, that's Kai's life story except dad didn't have a mistress." I was stuck at that point. That news first allowed me to stop crying and finally succeed at sniffing my snot back up my nose. I know, gross. “So, you and dad didn't have Kai? She isn't my “real” sister?" “Well legally she's your real sister but biologically, no, she isn't" I didn't really understand all those words, but I just had to ask one more question. “So you guys had ME, right? I'm your real daughter?" Before my mom could respond to my questions, my dad busted open the door, angry at my mom for whatever he thought she did to Kai, or whatever Kai told him she did. "Kim, why the fuck is Kai locked up in her room crying?" Sarcastically my mom said to my dad, “Well hello honey, and how was your day? Mine was fine, Kana's, not so much." My dad replied, “I can’t with the sarcasm Kim, what's up?" “Kai told Kana she was adopted and her real mom was strung out on Crack and she was your mistress." Now my dad is an extremely laid back type of guy, who never raised his voice at Kai or me when we were growing up. When my mom told him what Kai said to me, he sat down on the chair at the foot of their bed, put his elbow on the arm of the chair and then his head in his hand and looked down for about 20 seconds before he spoke again. He was always careful to think about what he wanted to say before he said it. He lifted his head up and moved his hand to allow his chin to rest. "Kai, come here!" My dad yelled; (so much for never raising his voice at us). My parents and Kai decided early on that they would tell me about Kai being adopted, as a family, when the time was right. The fact that Kai blatantly disrespected that wish pissed my dad off. When she finally came into the room where we all were, she had a smirk on her face. The smirk seemed malicious, like she had something up her sleeve. My parents should have known at that moment that it was time to give her up. "You think it's funny? There is nothing funny about the misery you put your sister through. That was the problem. Kai felt nothing, no compassion for any wrong thing she'd ever done. It was like her heart was removed from her chest and because of that, everything was a joke to her. Thank God I remembered this because I was beginning to feel badly for her. Now let's go back to London's house "You're full of shit Kai and I want you to leave me alone until my mom gets home." Before she could respond, my phone started to ring. My mom must have hung up or gotten disconnected. My heart started beating extremely fast when I saw who it was on the phone. "I will be at the Grant's house in five minutes," my dad said very calmly and then he hung up. At that point, there were one million thoughts going through my mind. What is he going to do to Mike? What is he going to do to Kai? Those were just a few thoughts dancing in my head. I pray he waits until we leave the Grant's. There's nothing worse than airing your family's dirty laundry in the streets, especially the streets of Chicago. "Kana who was it?" Kai struggled to ask. I wasn't sure if I should tell her it was dad or if I should just let her see. I then received a text from my mom saying, "Your dad is on the way to get you, and I told him everything." I realized then that there was no point in lying to her. "It is my dad, and he was on his way to get me." "Why did you say "my" dad? Does OUR dad know what's going on? Did you tell him? Did your mom tell him?" The waterworks began again. (Picture me rolling my eyes into another dimension. No, really, please do that now). You can't knock on the devil's door and start crying when he answers. I couldn't answer her because her cries were interrupted by Ms. Grant telling me my dad was at the door and that he seemed very anxious to go. I jumped up, grabbed my cell phone and headed towards the door. Kai, unsure of what she should do, hesitated to follow me to the door but proceeded to do so anyway.

CHAPTER 3:

I94

“Hey Daddy" I said with my head down. I was trying to avoid eye contact with him so he wouldn't think I was sad. Kai walked up to my dad and reached out for a hug. He hesitated to give her one but remembered where we were and extended his arms and gave her the church side hug (that was better than slapping her, if you ask me). My dad thanked Ms. Grant for allowing me to stay with them. “No problem, Smooth," she said. Of course since London and I had been best friends for almost ten years at that point, our parents were on first name/ nickname basis. My dad is 6'3”, very thin, always dressed to the 9's with a customized suit or linen outfit with some matching alligator shoes and has a way with women.

He's from Detroit so his tongue is slick and smooth (stay away from those Detroit men ladies, they will break your heart so sweet you'll end up falling harder than you did the first time). The guys on the block where my dad grew up gave him the name because of his demeanor and how he had the women in the neighborhood fighting over him. He'd handle the fighting women so smoothly that they'd become friends! Black people know we love us some nicknames. Anyway, after my parents divorced, my dad moved back to Detroit, leaving me to wonder where exactly we were headed. We had been in the car for about ten minutes going east on Interstate 94, which is the road you take to Detroit. Our silence dominated the atmosphere in the car. Can you imagine how fed up I was with this disturbing silence?

Finally, Kai asks where we were headed. "Granny's," my dad says casually as though my Granny doesn't live on the eastside of Detroit! I have school, dance practice, and this boy I just met that I cannot get enough of. What you mean "we" going to Detroit? I instantly asked him one thousand questions. "How long are we going to be there? Is Mom going to come get me? What's going on? Why do we have to go there?" I remembered my heart feeling like it was in my feet when my dad responded. "Ever since your mom met Mike, you and your sister have gone down a very bad path and I have to correct it." I started hyperventilating because I was crying so hard. I was hot and cold at the same time. "How in the fuck do I get penalized for this slut of a girl y'all got off the street? I was not consulted on bringing her into the family, and I should not be involved in what y'all do to correct her. My sister and I have been going down a very bad path? She went down the very bad path- not me." Now, had I said that to my mother, my teeth would have been in my hands! My dad understood my frustration and just answered me as though I didn't just come at him so disrespectfully. "Kai is going to live with her biological mother, and we are enrolling you in the high school around the corner from our house in Southfield."

That question and answer exchange between my dad and me created a very heated conversation between my dad and Kai. Kai began with, "You're taking me where?" My dad responded, "You heard me Kai." Kai yelled, "She's a crack head! I'm going to end up just like her if you take me there." Sarcastically my dad replied, "That's obviously what you want. You have blocked every attempt Kim and I have made to try to make your life better. You steal from us, treat Kana like shit, and this just in, you're fucking Kim's boyfriend." Kai pleaded, "Send me to boarding school or send me anywhere but there, please. I won't make it there (she began to cry). I will get killed or end up in jail. My dad's quick retort was "This is the path you chose! You're 17! Get your shit together!" Kai snapped back, "I'm calling Kim, There is no way she wants this to happen." My dad said laughingly (knowing the call wouldn't go through), "Please call her now." Kai pulled out her phone, dialed my mom's number and heard the following: "Your service has been temporarily suspended." I'm sorry but I couldn't hold in my laughter. Then I said, "That's what you get you silly goose!" I was sitting in the front seat of my dad's black Cadillac, (the big body, Detroit as fuck model), when Kai extended her arm to slap me in my face.

Pause,

What do you think happened next?

A. I turned around and slapped her back and my dad said, "Stop!"

B. I started crying and my dad put her out on the side of the road.

or

C. My dad pulled over so we could fight.

If you guessed C, you are absolutely right. We pulled off of the interstate onto Burr Street because we were in Indiana. If y'all thought I was gon' let somebody, anybody slap me and get away with it, you thought wrong.

I know you don't know me yet, but this is the first of many, I don’t play and I been waiting for a chance to fight her. When she slapped me, I turned around and slapped her back. She pulled me to the back seat with her so we were fighting in the back seat. My dad started yelling, “I am driving, cut that shit out." Once my dad noticed that we weren't going to stop and we were drawing blood, he pulled over. She busted my lip, and I gave her a nose bleed. When the car stopped moving, both Kai and I got out of the car. I jumped on her back and started hitting her in the head. What stupid bitch would hit the person they taught how to fight? I'm using all yo’ shit on you, Dumb Dumb. Kai failed at every attempt to get me off her back because I was holding on for dear life with my legs wrapped around her. She fell down to the ground and my dad pulled us apart. “That’s why I fucked EJ. He don't want yo’ young ass," Kai yelled as my dad was holding me back from getting to her. Let me remind you guys that we are just off the expressway on a street in Indiana, fighting.

Remember the guy I said I couldn't get enough of? That's EJ. He was three years older than me, a senior, and I was a freshman. My heart fell to my feet when she said that. I got loose from my dad and went and punched Kai in the face and said, "Round two bitch." She didn't expect me to punch her, because she was fixing her hair. She fell to the ground. You know I got on top of her and went to "town" on that face. It's a shame I had to fight my "sister" like that. She had it coming though, right? My dad pulled us apart again, as the police were pulling up because we were just off of the expressway acting like animals on Burr Street! Someone rode past rolling their window down to scream, "World Star!" "Stop before we all go to jail," my dad said as he pulled me from on top of Kai. The police said over the loudspeaker aggressively, "Get back in your vehicle, now." So we got our black asses back in the vehicle and the police drove off. Kai was sitting in the front and I was sitting in the back. I'll be damned if I let her sneak me again.

Kai's birth mom lived in Kalamazoo Michigan, two hours from Chicago and two hours from Detroit. Kai and I fell asleep after the expressway fight. I woke up to Kai's mother and my dad arguing about Kai staying with her. I thought it was going to be like at the end of Glitter when Mariah Carey took that long ass ride after Dice died, to go see her mother after all those years. That reunion was beautiful, this reunion wasn't that at all. Kai finally woke up and asked me where we were. "Yo' mama's house," I responded. "Why are they arguing? What the hell is going on?" I think her questions were rhetorical because she immediately opened the door and walked out after she asked them. I never met Katrina. I only saw her when she and Kai would face time. She still called Kai by the name she gave her at birth, Mellani.

The following conversation between Kai and her mother, made me want to run back to Chicago and thank my mother for the way she loved me. The way that Kai's mother spoke to her was filled with hate and disgust. Katrina barked, "Get back in the car Mellani! Smooth and I are talking." Kai responded, "About what? What's going on?" Katrina said, "About you staying here. I don't want you around my man either." Kai defensively said, "Nobody wants that crack head ass nigga but you Katrina and trust me, I don't want to be here either." Katrina bucked. "OK good, Getcho' triflin' ass back in the car den. I can't believe you did what they said you did. This is why I couldn't take care of you. You are the devil." Kai disputed, "No, just the daughter of "the devil!" Katrina was pissed at what Kai said and she sprinted toward Kai to attempt to fight her. My dad stopped Katrina mid-sprint. Since Katrina was strung out on drugs, she was very skinny and Kai would have beaten her ass. Kai sat on top of my dad's Cadillac laughing as my dad was trying to calm Katrina down. "Katrina, calm the fuck down. She is your daughter and needs you more than ever now. Get it together!" Katrina's husband, who wasn't Kai's father, (Kai's biological dad was in federal prison where he'd been for ten years because of credit card scams), walked outside with a shotgun and threatened to shoot us if we didn't leave. I began to feel badly for Kai, not because of her actions, but because of her genetics and her inability to fight off the inevitable. We left.

I woke up to the sounds of the road and the lights from the cars going west on Interstate 94. It was 3:00 AM and I didn't even remember falling asleep. Kai was in the front seat knocked out with her headphones in her ear. I looked at my dad through the rear view mirror and he seemed flustered, like something very complex was going through his head. He was probably thinking that Kai being in Detroit would embarrass him. My dad lived a "private" life in Detroit, with his girlfriend Lacey. He, his two siblings, my granny and late grandpa moved to Detroit from Alabama when my dad was three. At that time, segregation ran rampant. My granny was determined to give her family a better life. Then why move to Detroit, you ask? I know, I asked the same thing. My dad didn't like bringing any extra attention to him, so I know Kai being in Detroit would cause problems in his life. I received thirteen missed calls and six text messages from EJ on my sidekick 4G.

EJ:" Kana!!! Why are you not answering?"

EJ:"Kana “what the fuck” I been calling you for hours, if you don't wanna talk just say that!"

First of all, now that I know this nigga fucked my sister, I wanted nothing to do with him. OK ladies, I need to know how you think I should have handled this:

A. Curse him out and tell him to never call me again.

Or

B. Ask him if he and Kai slept together, because Kai could have been lying.

Well, since I was 14 years old I went with A. At the time I wasn't mature enough to successfully execute option B without doing option A eventually, so I decided not to waste any more time with him. I had to wait until my dad got out the car so that I could call EJ and cuss his ass out. Finally my dad parked in my granny's driveway (because her two cars are in the garage) and said nothing. Kai woke up from the sound of the door slamming. We just got on the road so we didn't have any bags. I forgot my book bag and the bag of clothes I had at London's house. You would think I would have gotten enough of forgetting bags. Remember what happened when I forgot my book bag at Mike's house? I told Kai to go in without me because I was going to sit in the car for a while. She rolled her eyes and went in. I knew she was afraid to be around my dad without me, because even though we hated each other, my dad's silence was super intimidating and very hard to deal with alone. Oh well, she put *herself* in that situation. There were three street lights outside. One was broken and the other one flickered. I sat in the car thinking about what I was going to say to EJ. I knew for sure I had to go off. I began to wonder if I should start off with, "Why the fuck is you concerned about me? You should only be concerned about Kai" or do I start off with, "Kai told me what y'all did. Did you use me to get to her?" I began to dial the number as he was calling me - what a coincidence. I flipped open the phone

Me: "Hello,"

EJ: "Why the fuck you not responding to me Kana? What's going on? Where are you?"

Me: "Why are you concerned about where I am? You blowing up Kai's phone too?"

EJ: "Why the fuck would I be calling your sister? What's wrong with you?"

Me: “Kai told me that y’all had sex. I have no idea why I thought you actually liked me. Why would you like me? I should have known you were using me to get to my sister.”

Before he had a chance to respond, I hung up and began crying. I’m not sure if I was crying because I should have listened to my cousin’s when they told me I was too young for him and that all he was going to do was play with me, or if I was crying because my entire family was in shambles and I had no idea how to help. It was easier for me to deal with EJ than my current family situation. So after the sixth time that he called, I called back. I had planned to just listen.

EJ: “Kana, I promise that never happened. She is fucking with your head and you're letting her! I really like you and I want to build with you. Where are you?”

Me: “I'm in Detroit with Kai and my dad.”

EJ: “I'm on my way!”

He hung up.

I tried to call back because I didn’t quite understand what he meant by, “I’m on my way.” Did he mean he was on his way to Detroit, where my father lived? Did he mean he was going to come to talk to his 14 year old daughter? To say what? “Oh sir, I really like your daughter and I’m just trying to get to know her.”

Granted EJ didn’t know that Kai said what she said about the two of them while she was in front of my dad, and the only thing my dad knew about “EJ” is that he slept with my sister and was supposed to like me. There is no way my dad would allow him to step foot in our home or allow me to go anywhere with him -not even on the front porch. I called him four times but he did not pick up. I had literally just got off of the phone with him about five minutes prior. The message had to get to him though, so I texted:

Me: “Kai told me that you and her had sex while she was in front of my dad.

I’m certain he’s going to have an issue with you coming here.” He texted back immediately, of course, I asked myself, how was this possible when he couldn't pick up the phone. I know that was the thought in y’all heads too, right?

EJ: “OK Kana, I’m on my way though. So please, figure out how I can see you. I’ll call you as soon as I get there - make it happen. Even at 14, I knew that a man who could take control like that, and make you do what he said even when he was in the wrong, was a man to run away from.

CHAPTER 4:

48 HOURS AFTER

"Kana!" My dad yelled extremely loudly from the doorway. "Yes Daddy?" I was sitting in the car with the lights off so I'm sure he panicked because he didn't see me. "Get in the house. Are you crazy?" He said to me as he walked off the porch toward the car. "I'm sorry Daddy. I just needed to clear my head." "It's 4:00 AM and this is Detroit, so you clear your head in the bathroom." I couldn't blame him for being so hostile because we did have a lot going on, and if I had come up missing that would have been the "icing on the cake." I understood where he was coming from, so I went in the house to my room and climbed into bed with all my clothes on. I threw the covers over my face. I prayed before I closed my eyes. "Lord, please protect my family from the demon that has surfaced and please help us escape with no scratches, Amen." Wishful thinking, right?

I woke up to the smell of bacon at around 11:30 AM. I checked my phone first, to see if anyone cared enough about me to see why I wasn't at school today or yesterday. There were a couple of texts from my crazy ass friend Frankie who was in my choir class. Our class had 45 students and she and I were the only Black girls.

Frankie: “Ummm, we said we would tell each other if we were going to skip class.”

“Girl is you alive? EJ done came up to me twice looking for you. So has Lil’Dre. You better contact yo’ hoes.”

“OK, now I'm worried. Where the fuck is you at!!!!”

“I haven't seen Kai either. Call me Kana!!!!!”

It made me happy that she was worried. I texted her back, “I’m OK Frankie, I'll call you soon." EJ told me he was on his way to Detroit. It only takes 4 hours to get to Detroit from Chicago so I began to worry. Instead of calling him, I went downstairs to eat. I passed Kai's room and she was still sleeping. I did not wake her up and tell her that the food was ready because she wouldn't have done that for me -petty I know. When I got downstairs, my dad and granny were at the table. My dad was reading a newspaper, and my granny was watching the cooking channel on the TV mounted on the wall over the microwave. I hadn't seen my granny in a few weeks and I didn't know if my dad had told her what was going on, so I proceeded into the kitchen, with caution. "Good morning Kana, how did you sleep?" Before I could respond to my dad, my granny said, "I'm so happy you and Kai decided to spend your fall break here with us. It's so good having you both around." I knew

then, my granny knew nothing! We were not on fall break. School had just started. I knew my dad told her that so he wouldn't have to tell her exactly what was going on. In a way this scenario was great! In a way this scenario was not great. My granny was a very observant person, she would have noticed that my dad and I were standoffish with Kai. She would have called a family meeting. My granny is a real Southern Bell, meaning that she is extremely family- oriented. She believes in nipping situations in the bud before they get in the streets. Oh child! If she only knew. My dad stood up, told me to sit down in his seat and he would make my plate. My granny made us bacon, scrambled eggs with American cheese, waffles, and grits with butter. She made this every time Kai and I came to visit. We would always sit at the kitchen table to eat. There were always the same rules: no phones, no TV unless everyone wanted to watch it, and you had to be a part of whatever conversation was going on. "I'm happy to be here granny! We can't go that long without seeing each other again." The house was so old that you heard everything that happened upstairs, downstairs in the kitchen. I knew Kai was up because I heard the wood floors squeak. They were so loud. Anyway, she walked downstairs, came into the kitchen as if she literally rolled out of bed, and she looked like shit. She didn't speak to me, or my dad, or my granny. She went right to the cabinet over the stove where the plates were and grabbed two. We were appalled that she still hadn't said anything to us, so we continued to watch to see how long it was going to take her to speak. When Kai first walked into the kitchen, my granny stood up to give her a hug. Then Kai proceeded to walk past Granny and ignored her open arms to make her plate. My granny's smile slowly turned into a frown. Finally I spoke up and said "Kai you're being rude." She turned around, looked my dad, my granny, and me in our eyes and began laughing. She then turned back around, finished fixing her plate, and walked out of the kitchen. Kai is a bitch to everyone except my granny. It had gotten to the point where my parents and I would complain about Kai to Granny but Kai had her so fooled that she never believed us. My granny asked my dad what we had done to Kai for her to act that way. My dad didn't want my granny to panic so he told her Kai was upset about a boy. Whose grandma would accept that and move on? (Nobody's Black grandma). My granny excused herself from the table and went upstairs to Kai's room to check on her.

"Knock knock. Kai, can I come in?" Kai didn't respond. My granny opened the door because I mean, it was her house. She walked in the room as Kai was sitting on the bed texting. Kai didn't acknowledge the fact that my granny had entered the room. She sat at the foot of her bed and asked Kai to put the phone down so they could talk. She began by asking, "Kai, what's going on? You're never this distant." Kai answered "Oh, they didn't tell you?" Granny replied "Your dad said it was about a boy, but I know my baby would never let a boy alter her emotions like that." Kai yelled "A boy!? Ha Ha they lied to you. I don't want to talk about it. Can you please leave me alone and close my door?"

Kai picked her phone back up to continue to text. The entire time my granny was talking to Kai, Granny was calm, she didn't raise her voice, not even once. The moment Kai asked my granny to close the door in her own house, Granny went off, but in a "Phylicia Rashad" type of way. Her voice still monotone, she got very close to Kai, snatched the phone out of her hand, put a smile on her face and said, "Oh Baby, I'm not sure what you're going through, but don't you ever in your life disrespect me the way that you just did. I am not too old to teach you a lesson. You are in my home which I have graciously allowed you to feel as if it were your home for your entire life. I don't deserve this treatment and more importantly, I won't accept it. To me it sounds like boy issues. A grown woman would handle her shit and not let her entire life be affected by one situation. However, I forgot you are not a grown woman. Grow up my baby." Kai's mouth dropped, she had nothing to say. My granny gave her cellphone back to her, gave her a kiss on the cheek and walked out of her room, leaving the door open. Something told me not to do what I'm about to tell y'all I did. I walked into Kai's room about 15 minutes after my granny left. "Are you okay?" I asked Kai very hesitantly. "I'm OK Kana. What do you have to say?" "What's going on with you Kai? Why did you do that to my mom and why were you so disrespectful to Granny?" Kai turned and looked out of the window that was to the right of her bed and said, "Kana, you're too young to understand this, but I love Mike and we are going to start a family together." She smiled and began to rub her stomach. As if this shit couldn't get any worse, the bitch was alluding to the fact that she was pregnant. I should have gone downstairs and minded my damn business. Instead, I paused and stared at Kai for about 30 seconds. I parted my lips to speak but nothing would come out. "I know that you're going to tell Kim. That's why I told you. She had no idea how to handle a man like that anyway." Kai said as she got up and began to pack up the clothes she kept at my granny's house.

Shocked and at a loss for words, I started walking out of the room and her phone began to ring. She dropped everything and picked up her phone. I'm assuming Mike paid for her phone to be cut back on because by the way she answered, I could tell the call was from him. “Hi Baby, what took you so long to call me?" she asked in a very whiny voice. I walked extremely slowly toward the door so I could hear the conversation. "Wait, hold on. Kana please get out." She caught on to me, so I left the room and closed the door. I went into my room to find my phone so that I could tell my mom the news I had just received. I had 15 missed calls from EJ and five angry texts.

EJ:”I know damn well you see me calling you.”

EJ: “Kana, I'm here in Detroit at my boy’s auntie crib. Let me know where you are, I'm coming to get you!”

EJ: “I came out here to see you and I'm not leaving until I do.”

EJ: "I promise I did not do what Kai is saying, I would never do that to you, and I hope that you aren't ignoring me because of her."

EJ: "KANA!!!!!!!!!!!!!!!!!!!!!!!!!!!!!!!!"

I couldn't deal with EJ at that moment. I had to call my mom, and tell her that Mike got Kai pregnant. I hadn't spoken to my mom since she told me that my dad was on the way to get me so I didn't know where she was or what she was doing. I remember calling four times before I actually got through to her. When she finally answered she said, "What's up NaNa?" in a hurry- up- and- talk, kind of way. Before I could tell her the news, I heard Mike in the background, "What do you want to eat Kim?" "Where are you Ma? Is that Mike?" I remembered being so disgusted because I knew she was with him before I asked because his voice was very distinctive. "Yes it is Kana. Can I call you back? Is everything OK?" She asked, rushing me off the phone.

"No! Everything is not OK. Kai said she is pregnant with Mike's baby. I was just in the room with her when they were on the phone. He had her phone turned back on. Hello, Ma are you there?" I heard the dial tone because she hung up on me. I sat on my bed trying to figure out my next move. At that point in my life, I felt as if I could go to no one. I didn't want to tell my dad what Kai had told me because I knew he would put her out and she had absolutely nowhere to go. When my granny left Kai's room, she went to the casino, where she always goes to clear her head. "I have to get away from them," is what I said out loud- with no thought. Immediately I called EJ and told him to come get me. I didn't care about my dad finding out where I was going or who I was going with. At 14 years old, all that drama was driving me crazy. Listen y'all, it had only been two days since I caught Mike and Kai in the bed together, ONLY TWO!

The first thing I said to EJ when I ran out of the house and got in the car with him was, “Please take me back to Chicago. My mother is in trouble!” Perplexed as to why we had to go back to Chicago, he asked, “What are you talking about Baby? I just drove four hours to see you.” I don’t understand what more I had to say other than my mother was in trouble. He should have said “say no more. Let’s go.” Since that wasn’t his response, I instantly got an attitude. It was easier to be angry with him than to face my reality. Yelling, I said, “Why the fuck do I have to explain anything, I said my mom is in trouble. We have to go now, please!” I never raised my voice at him as much as I had since Kai told me what they did. I was always extremely sweet to him and just basically star struck around him. He could tell that I was serious and something had come over me. “OK, Kana let’s go. Do you have to go back in to get...?” “Just go now, before my dad comes out,” I interrupted him. He had his cousin in the car with him, who I didn’t even notice because he was very quiet in the back seat. “Hey Kana, how are you doing?” I turned around and gave him the meanest look I could think of for asking that dumb- ass question. Very sarcastically I said, “Oh, I’m just peachy and excited to get back to Chicago to see if this man killed my mother!” EJ was shocked at what I said and immediately took his eyes off the road and began asking questions. “Kana what’s going on? What do you mean if this man killed your mother? Please let me know so I can help you.” He asked calmly. His voice showed concern and anger. Do I tell him what’s going on? I really don’t know that much about him. I’ve heard stories about him. I know he’s from a very rough hood in Chicago but I’m uncertain as to what he could do to help with this situation. Boy did I underestimate him! “Kana! WHAT THE FUCK IS GOING ON?” he yelled. I went off in daze thinking about the possibilities of what could happen if I told him everything that was going on. “I’m sorry. Long story short: Kai has been fucking my mom’s boyfriend, I walked in on them, told my mother, fought Kai on the side of the road, met her crack head biological mother, and found out Kai is pregnant by Mike- all in two days." We weren't on the expressway yet when I started telling the story. EJ stepped on the brakes extremely fast in the middle of Jefferson. If you've ever been in downtown Detroit, you know that's one of the busiest streets in the city. Thank God we didn't get into a car accident. "Aye cuz, drive for me," EJ hopped out the driver's seat and asked me to climb in the back with him. He immediately pulled out his phone and began dialing someone's number. "Go to Kana's house and check on her mother, now. I'm finna text you the address. I'm driving from Detroit, and I'll be there in about three hours," EJ said really fast to whomever he was on the phone with. "Kana, here's my phone. Text my homie your address." I guess I was moving too slowly, because he yelled, "KANA, RIGHT NOW!" "OK EJ don't yell," I said as I took the phone and did as I was told. When I gave EJ his phone back, he took my hand and pulled it to his lips. "I got you now Baby, Go to sleep. When you wake up everything will be better." I'll never forget those words.

PART TWO:

By now, you've finished your tall glass of champagne. You've probably finished the bottle. Pop another. Think about part one. Prepare for part two. It's deep.

Enjoy,

Modi

CHAPTER 5 :

UNIT # UNKNOWN

I woke up scared shitless because I was in a queen size bed, alone. When I fell asleep, I was in the car with EJ. I got out the bed to see if someone was in the house with me. I opened the door to a very nice living room, fully furnished with earth like tones. To the right of the living room was a kitchen with granite counter tops and white faux fur bar stools. At that point I still had no idea where I was, but I was thankful I didn't wake up in a Motel 6 with strangers. I had to call EJ because it was getting creepy in that nice- ass apartment by myself. I looked for pictures thinking it would tell me where I was, but of course there were no pictures. I went back into the room to look for my phone. Thank God it was on the nightstand to the right of the bed. When I looked at my phone, there were 50 missed calls from my dad, 45 from my mom as well as 100 texts from Kai.

Also there was a text from EJ telling me to call him when I woke up. Of course I called him first.

EJ: “What’s up Lil’ Baby, You finally up huh?”

Kana: “First off, where the fuck is you and where the fuck am I?”

EJ: “Do you like it?”

Kana: “Do I like what?”

EJ: “The apartment that you’re in.”

Kana: “EJ stop playing with me and tell me where you are.”

EJ: “Open the door.”

OK, now I’m starting to get irritated. What is this man up to, more important, what I have gotten myself into? I walked past the kitchen door, and I stood up on my tippy toes because I'm 4’1”, to look through the peephole. It was EJ looking good as

fuck in a pair of grey Polo Ralph Lauren sweatpants. "Hurry up and open the door girl. You know it's me," he said through the door in a Jody from Baby Boy type of way. I opened the door, he picked me up, spun me around, kissed me, and put me back on the floor. "You are so beautiful in the morning Kana."
Immediately, I remembered I was in a foreign place with the man I couldn't get enough of. I had to bring myself back to life and find out what the hell was going on.

I began the conversation by asking EJ what was going on and where we were. I thought we were going to see about my mom at Mike's house. Instead, I woke up alone in a place that I had never been. EJ repeated the question he asked me on the phone, "Do you like this place Kana? You never gave me an answer." As I looked around the place I said, "I love it. It's so nice. I wish I could stay but I'm sure by now my entire family is looking for me and I couldn't even begin to tell them where I am."
He passionately stated, "Call them and tell them you're at home."

Here we go again with the fairytale, pinch yourself Kana because this cannot be real, you are for sure still in the car, I thought to myself and proceeded to pinch myself. EJ saw me pinch myself and he laughed and said, "it's real baby." His aura was so sure, I had to remind him that I was 14 and my parents would never allow me to live with him. When I said that, it upset him and he bucked back "What they gon do? Take me to court? I can tell them your mother's boyfriend got your sister pregnant. It's cool Baby. I told you, I got you and no one would hurt you again." Finally I answered, "Great, but this is the real world. What do I say to them? How do I continue a normal life? I can't drive. Are you going to take me to school? I don't have a job. Are you going to provide for me?" In mid-sentence, EJ got up from the couch, grabbed me, picked me up, took me to the room, laid me on the bed and began to unzip the pink Juicy Couture track suit I had on. He whispered into my ear "Relax NaNa, I got you. I'll never leave you." He started feeling on my thighs, took his hand up through the shirt I had on and started feeling on the boobs that I did not have. I stopped him and said, "I'm not ready for this." In my head I thought he was going to flip and tell me he was taking me back to my messed up family. Instead he said, "OK, we will wait until you are ready." He gave me a kiss on my forehead then handed me my phone. Calmly he said, "Call your mom, tell her you want to talk, and to meet up with her." "And you think it'll be easy huh? I just call my Black mother and say, "Hey Ma, I'm going to live with this 18 year- old boy that I'm crazy about. I know you've never met him and actually I just met him, but yea, this is happening." Do you really think she will just say, "OK NaNa, I'll visit?" You know we just light skinned, right? My Mamma is Black as fuck," I said to him very sarcastically. He laughed, pushed my hair out of my face, and said, "You worry too much. I said I got you. Don't you trust me?" I smiled and thought to myself, I do trust him, and that's the scary part. What the fuck are you doing Kana? You are 14 years old and you're going to live with this man, alone? Yes because I believe him when he says, I got you, I'll never leave you." I think it's his eyes; his big brown eyes, the scars under his eyes that tell me he's been through some shit and that he can handle some shit. He better be able to handle anything because my mom is about to go ape shit on him and actually me too for that matter. After he said that, I took the phone and went into the bathroom. I didn't want him to hear my mother curse me out, and remind him of how old I was. My mom picked up on the first ring, screaming, "Kana Lanae Steele! Where the fuck are you? I have been calling and texting you. I was worried. Now that you've called me and I know you're alive, when I see you 'Ima' beat yo' ass. I interrupted, "Ma, please just hear me out. I am safe and very well taken care of." She interjected, "You're 14 Kana. You do not have the luxury of doing whatever you want to do. As a matter of fact, where are you? I'm coming to get you now!" I started crying and could barely respond to her. She wouldn't let me talk. She just kept yelling. I assumed EJ could hear her so he came in and took the phone from me and hung up. He turned my phone off. I was absolutely appalled that he did that.

"EJ, why did you do that? If she calls the police what are we going to do? I am a minor," I said frantically. He looked at me with the stale face and said, "You starting to piss me off. I told you I would take care of you. Now sit back and let me." Sharply I said, "Sorry EJ, but it's not that fucking simple. I need to tell them where I am. I need to know what's going to happen to my sister. I need to know if my mom and Mike are still together. I told you all the things going on in my life and you think the best thing to do is run?" He could tell my whole demeanor had changed so he softened up and said, "Kana I'm not trying to upset you Baby. I told you I'll never leave you. I'm going to protect you. If it will make you happy, we can go to your mom's boyfriend's house. You need to get your things anyway."

I began to stare at him for three reasons:

1. The man is fine as fuck. Let me elaborate.. He's 5'9" caramel complexion, rocks a low fade, and very nice hair. He kind of puts you in the mindset of Aladdin, if he were human and thuggish. Hell of a combination I know, but ladies, I bet you pictured him.
2. I'm trying to figure out why he thinks this process is going to go so smoothly.
3. What does he see in my young ass that makes him want to live with me and take care of me?

Something inside of me was dying to see it through. I just had to know what he had planned for when we got to Mike's house. I asked him if he was ready to go. He said, "Born ready Lil' Baby." So off we went.

CHAPTER 6:

OUR APARTMENT

I was sweating profusely. My hands and feet were shaking uncontrollably in the car ride over to Mike's house. EJ's apartment wasn't far from Mike's house, maybe 15 minutes away. EJ placed his hand on my thigh and said, "Relax Baby. It's going to be OK." EJ's very soft voice gave me a feeling in between my legs that I had never felt before. I looked up at him and he smiled. Did I mention that he had perfectly white teeth? At that moment I knew I had gotten myself into some deep shit and what was worse, I liked it! Suddenly, I was not scared anymore. I felt like with him next to me, I could conquer the world. But first, I had to conquer my mom. When we pulled up in front of Mike's house, there were two Yukon Denali trucks out front that did not look familiar. "I have no idea who this is in these cars. Maybe we should go," I said to EJ.

To my surprise he started laughing. "Dem my brothers Lil' Baby. We good," he said as he reached over the center counsel of his black Escalade truck to unfastened my seatbelt. "Come on. Let's go in," he said like it was an arcade or the circus. "Hold the fuck up. Why are your so-called brothers here? What do you have planned?" I asked, completely confused. As I was talking, six guys hopped out of the trucks, three from each. They all went to EJ's window. He put up his index finger signaling them to wait a minute. He took off his seat belt and turned his body towards me and said, "Baby, I told you I had you. But, we gotta do this now. We can't sit out here long enough for me to explain what's about to happen." "Don't put your hands on my mother and make sure they don't." My voice was shaky when I said that because I was so uncertain of the events that were about to take place. I took a deep breath and got out the car.

We walked up the three steps to the front porch of Mike's house, rang the doorbell and waited until someone answered the door.

Mike's doors were frosted glass so you could only see the silhouette of the person coming towards the doors. I could tell it was my mom by the curves of her hips and the attitude in her walk. EJ looked at me, grabbed my hand and kissed it. My mom saw that and began to shout as she was opening the door. "Kana! What the fuck and who the fuck is this? Get your ass in here now!" She attempted to pull me into the house but was interrupted by EJ's assertive greeting, "Good afternoon, I'm Eric, Kana's Boyfriend, and she is coming to live with me. We are just here to get her stuff." "Boyfriend?" I thought to myself. That was the first time I heard him refer to himself as my boyfriend. That did it. I was riding with him no matter which way this conversation went. My mom started laughing and blurted out, "Over my dead body, she is. How old are you? You know what, don't answer that. NaNa get your ass in here before I embarrass you in front of this little boy!" "We here to get my stuff ma, I do not want to be a part of this screwed up family. He does something horrible like sleep with your daughter and you still won't leave him." My mother angrily replied, "He is not the problem and she is not my daughter. She is the problem. That's why she is back at Katrina's." "But Ma, Katrina told my dad that Kai couldn't stay there. Kai is still in Detroit at my dad's house. You would have known that if you weren't so up Mike's ass and cared about your family more. Don't you see what he's doing to you?" Wow! She smacked me right upside my face. "You are not grown. You are entirely too young to understand what's going on. More importantly, you're too young to move out of my house without my permission. So like I said get your ass in here and now you can't ever see him again." Calmly EJ stated, "No Ma'am. She is leaving with me, sorry." "Aye," he yelled at the boys by the cars. "Let's do it." The six guys walked up the steps and before they could walk in the house, my mom hollered for Mike. "Mike! Kana, really? I'm your mother and you're going to just leave me, to go and stay with this random hoodlum. Also, why are these guys here?" EJ saw that Mike was walking down the stairs so he yelled "Kana! Show them where your stuff is so we can go." Mike walked down the stairs with a very disturbed look on his face and said, "Who the fuck are these niggas in my house?"

At first, I started to feel like I was in the wrong for leaving my mom there with the fucking devil. Then she smacked me and all that shit went out the window. I couldn't wait to get my belongings and get out of there. As EJ and I started to walk off the porch to the car, my mom yelled, "Kana, if you don't get your ass back in here, I'm calling the police." Before I knew it, I sarcastically responded, "Yea please call them on Mike since he raped my sister." I saw my mother's face just drop and tears starting to form. She hated the police anyway, I knew she wouldn't call them. I pointed to my room that was on the first floor to the left of the kitchen. The six guys walked passed my mom and Mike to my room to get my things. EJ grabbed my hand and we walked off the front porch to his car. I turned around to look at my mom. She looked as if I had shot her in her heart. I got in the car with no remorse, EJ immediately drove off. I felt a rush, like I could really do anything with this man by my side. I knew he had my back and there was no turning back. "Kana and EJ sitting in the tree, K- I- S- S-I- N- G, first comes love then comes marriage, then comes Kana with a baby carriage" I was so in my thoughts and feelings that I didn't realize he was going 100 miles on the freeway with Plies " Bust it Baby" playing extremely loud on the radio. "What you thinking about Lil' Baby?" he asked after he turned the music down. "What makes you want to do this? Why do you want to save me?" I asked, with my hand under my chin batting my eyelashes and blushing. "I see something in you I've never seen before. You're beautiful, smart and even though this is happening with your family, I know you come from good stock. This tragedy could change you and the person I know you're going to become.

I want to save you so that doesn't happen." Ladies, how come no one told me older boys prey on freshman? He grabbed my hand and kissed it. I had no more questions after that, I trusted him with everything in me.

"Let me see your phone?" Without thinking, I handed it to him. He rolled his window down and tossed it out. I screamed, "NO!! Why would you do that?" "Look in the bag in the back seat," he said calmly. I turned around and there was a T-Mobile bag on floor. In there was a brand new pink Motorola Razr. "What's this?" I asked with an attitude because I was still mad that he threw my phone out the window with no warning. "I got you a new phone. Your mom was going to turn yours off as a way to get you to come back home." He made so much sense when he said that. I sat back and took the phone out and saw it was already on. EJ told me to put his number in the phone and that his number was the only number that mattered. "Can we just get married now?" I said as I kissed him on his cheek. We were in the garage of his apartment building now, or should I say our apartment. Yea, "our apartment," I like the way that sounds. When we got into the apartment, his phone rang. "At the door," the man on the phone said. EJ went to open the door and it was the six guys that got my stuff from Mike's house. They came in with black garbage bags and tons of my shoes. "My mom didn't try to stop you?" I asked. "At first she did. She was crying and screaming at us. But fat boy grabbed her and carried her upstairs and told us to hurry up and get the fuck out his house." I knew they weren't lying because Mike hates me. He was probably overly excited that I wanted to move out, so he could manipulate my mom without any interference. EJ showed me my side of the closest and the drawers in the bathroom that were mine so that I could start putting my clothes up. "You ready EJ?" One of the guys asked. "Yea, hold on," EJ said. "Where are you going?" I asked. "I got to make this run with them real quick, I'll be right back. I ordered you a pizza. It should be here in about ten minutes." He gave me a kiss on the forehead and ran out the door. I was still on a high so I really didn't care that he left. It would give me time to really process what just took place. The pizza came in ten minutes like he said. It was Beggars deep dish cheese pizza. When we first started talking I told him it was my favorite. This sealed the deal. He for sure had me at this point. I texted him "You really listen when I talk. Are you real?" He texted back immediately, "Only for you". It was only 4:00PM. I was extremely tired so I ate a few slices, turned the TV on in the bedroom and fell asleep. I was so comfortable nothing could take this feeling away. Well, not yet at least.

CHAPTER 7:

THE POINT OF NO RETURN

I woke up from my nap at around 10:30 PM, alone with no missed calls. I called EJ to see where he was, but he didn't pick up. I started to unpack my stuff to get my mind off of where he could be. That was only making me think harder about where he was because it was so much stuff. I was so confused on why I was putting my things up by myself. I texted him at 11:00 PM "Where are you?" He texted back immediately, "On my way home now." Why couldn't you answer the phone though? I should have asked him that right? Remember I'm 14 and have no idea how to handle this situation. So, of course I said nothing but, "OK, hurry please. I miss you." I put the phone down and continued putting my stuff up in the closet. There was a shoe box on my side of the closet that I wanted to move over to his side. I opened the box to see what was in it because it seemed heavier than a pair of shoes.

There were three guns in it. I sat and stared at them because I had never seen a real gun in person before. I think I stared at the guns for about ten minutes. I didn't even hear the door open. All I heard was, "What the fuck are you doing?" EJ yelled as he saw what I was looking at. "Oh I'm sorry. This box was on my side and I was trying to move it," I said kind of startled. I just got up and left the closet.

Who is this man, why does he have three guns? Seriously, what have I gotten myself into? These are just a few questions I asked myself as I went to sit on the couch in the front room. EJ came to sit next to me with the box of guns. "It's a lot of things about me you don't know. It's a lot I don't want you to know. Since we live together now I want you to know where some things are and how to use these" as he uncovered the box and pointed to the guns. "Here is a key. There is always a thousand dollars in the top drawer in a band aid box in the kitchen. That's yours for whatever you need."

After he said that, he picked one of the guns up and emptied it so there were no bullets in it. He handed it to me and I picked it up by the handle like a dirty sock. My eyes were focused. He laughed at me and stood up and got behind me. He wrapped his arms around me so that we were both holding the gun. He pushed his pelvis very close to my behind. I got weak in the knees (at the moment I absolutely understood what SWV was singing about). Then he whispered in my ear, "hold it like this Lil' baby, strong and firm, eyes open, point and aim then pull the trigger." He stepped back while I still had the gun in my hand and said, "You look so "gangsta" holding that, like my ride or die chick." I laughed and all of a sudden became the Bonnie to his Clyde. I mean the way I was holding the gun and making shooting sounds, you would have thought I was a professional. "OK Lil' Baby put it down. Use it when you have to." I'm sure he could tell I was getting carried away. The truth is that I loved the way he looked at me when I had his gun in my hand. I loved him calling me his ride or die chick. I would do anything to keep that title.

"Let's watch a movie," he said as he walked into the bedroom. Of course I caught an attitude when he said that because he knew I still had to put my stuff up. "I have to find something to wear to school tomorrow." "Look on the kitchen table," he said nonchalantly as he laid across the bed flipping through the channels. I walked from the living room that was to the left of the kitchen to the brown table that was set up like Thanksgiving dinner. The table settings made me wonder who decorated his place. Every inch was very detailed like it had a woman's touch. In the center of the table was a Jordan shoe box and a bag from True Religion with a pair of jeans and a white shirt to match. I opened the shoe box and it was the brand new Jordan "6 Rings". My mom would never buy me Jordan's. She said they were too ghetto for pretty girls to wear. I wanted these particular ones so bad because everyone at school had them. I screamed, ran in the room, and jumped in the bed on top of EJ. I kissed him and before I knew it, yea, I lost my virginity because I got some Jordans. My pussy was only worth one hundred and fifty dollars (somebody come smack the shit out me). It lasted for about 30 minutes. I use to listen to Kai and her friends talk about losing their virginity and they made it seem like it was going to be fairytales and roses. They failed to mention that I would bleed, cry, and be sore as fuck for days. I was embarrassed because I bled so much. I thought something was wrong with me. "There's so much blood. You broke it," I cried the ugly girl cry. EJ wrapped his arms around me. "It's OK Kana. Stop crying," he said as he got up and went to the bathroom. When I heard the water running, I thought, Oh no, he's got to wash my blood off of him. I wish I could spin myself into the ground like Rumpelstiltskin.

My face was in the pillow when he came back and took my hand to lead me to the bathroom. He drew a bath for me. "Sit in here for a minute baby Relax. I'll change the sheets," he said as he helped me step into the bathtub. I stayed in the tub for about 30 minutes. I forgot about Mike, my mom, my dad, Kai, and school. The only thing I could think about was EJ, how I never wanted to be without him and I hoped this didn't turn him off from me. I got out the tub, stepped on the grey memory foam floor mat, picked up the towel he laid out on the chair for me, wrapped it around me and went into the room where EJ was waiting to hand me one of his t -shirts to sleep in. "Lay down Kana. There is nothing to be embarrassed about. It's me and you forever" he said as we climbed into bed. He pulled me close and wrapped his arms around me. I knew then why Kai said I was too young to comprehend sex. My emotions were everywhere and I honestly couldn't take it. I knew one thing though. He had me and there was no turning back.

CHAPTER 8:

C- HALL

"Bitch where have you been?" Frankie screamed when she saw me. "Girl there's not enough time in this class to fill you in. What you been up to? That's probably easier." Before she could answer, Kai came to my class and signaled for me to come out. I was actually happy to see her at school. "Hold on Frankie. Let me see what my sister wants. Mr. Kino, can I be excused please?" My choir director loved me so of course he said yes when I asked. Frankie and I sat right in front so it took me no time to get to the door. I hugged Kai and started crying. My emotions were still everywhere so the simplest things caused me to cry. I had absolutely no control over them. She was shocked that I was crying, but she started crying too. "What is going on Kana? You just left me in Detroit and your phone is disconnected? Fill me in please." She seemed genuinely concerned. My sensitive ass was ready to spill all the beans. "Please don't tell anyone Kai. You're still my sister despite what's going. Please don't let me down," I said really believing she wouldn't.

"EJ came and got me from Detroit. We went to Mike's so I could get my things. My mom was there saying that She and Mike are going to stay together so I left her there." Before I could finish telling Kai what happened, she started yelling, "No the fuck they are not together. That's my man. I'm having his baby. I'm going to beat her ass." I was shocked at the audacity of her comfort level while she was telling me she was going to beat my mother's ass. I just had to swing on her. Before I knew it, we were in the middle of C- hall fighting. The security guards ran to us and separated us. "I bet I get that nigga of yours again. You and your mother think y'all are so perfect that y'all can have anybody. I took Mike from her. Bet I take EJ from you," she yelled as the security guard held her. I wasn't as rowdy and upset as she was so the security guard didn't have to hold me. As I was about to run over by the lockers where the security guards had placed her to punch her again, the boy that I was kind of talking to before I met EJ, Lil' Dre', walked up and grabbed me. "Kana stop!" he yelled. "Why were you and your sister just fighting? Where have you been? What is going on with you?" I began thinking to myself, why in the fuck would he ask me all those questions expecting a genuine answer right at the time? Lil' Dre' was a sophomore. He was a very nice guy. He was super smart and came from a really wealthy family. Where they got that wealth is unbeknownst to me. He and his two older brothers were the people to see at school for weed. Lil' Dre' wasn't as rough around the edges as EJ was but you could tell he's been through some tough times by the way he carried himself and the way he spoke. Lil' Dre' was definitely a better candidate for me. He met my mom a few times. She loved him. My mom would pick him up and we would have dates in the backseat of her CLS 500 Benz. He was also on the basketball team so my mom went to a few games with me. I abruptly stopped picking up the phone for Lil' Dre when I met EJ. My mind was entirely too consumed with everything about EJ. Since I hadn't spoken to Lil' Dre' since I went MIA on him, my response was vague "family issues," I said as I started crying. I literally just couldn't stop crying. He grabbed my arm and pulled me closer to him. We sat down on the benches as security walked to the dean's office with Kai. I told them she attacked me so I didn't have to go with them. Lil'Dre' allowed me to rest my head on his shoulder as he rubbed the back of my hair. I absolutely forgot where I was and what I was doing, more importantly who I was doing it with. He had tissue in his pocket, I lifted my head off his shoulder to wipe my eyes and blow my nose. I think God was on my side because at that exact moment, EJ ran over to where we were. Word got around school so fast and my phone was on silent so I didn't hear that he was texting me. As he was walking up, I stood up to greet him. I think that EJ must have thought it was something more than it was, or he was told it was something more because when he got close to us he punched Lil' Dre' in the face. Before Lil' Dre' could hit him back, I stood in front of EJ and attempted to push him back away before security came back and saw what was going on. I jumped on him wrapped my legs around his waist and my arms around his neck and whispered in his ear, " We have to get out of here before they call my mother and the police get involved. Please let's just go." He helped me get down and I grabbed his hand to guide him out of the door. EJ couldn't have just walked away before saying something slick to Lil' Dre'. "Stay away from my girl lil' ass nigga." Lil' Dre' let us get all the way to the door and then he said as he was laughing, "So what, y'all got a sister wives situation going on? You cool with him fucking your sister on the side Kana? I thought more of you shorty." We were so close to the door I could smell outside. I could smell freedom. EJ couldn't take that he said that and what was worse, neither could I. I turned and looked at EJ and my eyes began to water. Here I go again with this punk ass crying, I thought to myself. EJ could tell that bothered me so he had to say something. He grabbed my hand, smiled and yelled to Lil' Dre' "You know where we live, pull up". Lil' Dre' was feeling himself I guess and he said, "We? Kana, if I had known you were for sale, I woulda bought ya sooner." Pause, I absolutely hate when people quote movies to be funny. Nick Cannon said that in "Love Don't Cost a Thing" right before Christina Milian hurt his feelings and exposed his lame ass. Since Lil' Dre' caused us to create a scene in C-Hall again, I had to pull a Christina Milian. EJ, up until this point, had my back. If it were true about him and Kai, that was no place for me to check him on it, nor for me to ask Lil'Dre' to elaborate. "You're just mad because I don't want you anymore, I actually thought more of you too. I didn't think you would gossip and spread rumors. That's a female trait." EJ and I were still holding hands when I felt a tear fall on my cheek. I immediately turned around and yanked his hand with me. The hallway to C -hall led to the parking lot where EJ parked his car. When we got close to the car, away from where people could see us, I dropped his hand. I walked faster than him to the car and yelled, "Open the fucking door." He knew to open the door immediately.

As soon as he started the car, I reached over and turned the car off. "Kana, I don't know why they keep saying I did that. I would never do that to you. I love you Kana. Can't you see that?" he said while staring in my eyes trying to convince me he didn't have sex with Kai. "Can you imagine how it makes me feel to hear that, for the second time? Do you even know what happened? Why I was over there with him?" I said as the tears start rolling down my eyes. (I don't know about y'all but I'm damn sure tired of crying at this point). He leaned over, wiped my eyes with his hand, kissed me on the forehead and said, "We can talk about it when we get home." I really didn't want to be around him but I knew I couldn't go to Mike's house. "Can you take me to London's house please? I really just need to be around a friend right now," I said as I started putting my seatbelt on.

"Kana, don't start that shit please. What do I have to do? I can talk to Kai and tell her to stop spreading that dumb ass lie, I'll do anything? Please don't leave me!" he said as he was reaching to take my seatbelt off. I looked up at him very confused and said, "What are you talking about? I said I just wanted to talk to my friend, I'm not leaving you and I absolutely don't want you talking to Kai ever, about anything. I am going to give you one last chance to tell me the truth. Where does this even stem from? If you tell

me now, I promise I will never bring it up again. I just honestly want to know the truth so I'm better prepared to defend myself."

"I told you the truth. I never ever touched her. I don't like her, I only have eyes for you," he said as he kissed my hand. For some reason, I knew he was lying but I wanted to believe he was telling the truth so I tricked myself into believing him. I still wanted to go to London's house. "OK baby, Thank you for telling me the truth. Please take me to London's!" "Kana, OK fine if you insist but I'm picking you up," he said as he put his seatbelt on and started the car back up. "I'll ride home from school with you tomorrow. I'm overly emotional because I just lost my mother, my virginity and fought my sister again. I have to talk to someone who understands me and won't judge me. I promise I'm not saying that's what you do. I just really need to speak to someone about you, who isn't you. Please understand," I said, praying he would understand. "OK, Kana. Call me if you want me to come get you and I promise I will," he said as he pulled out of the parking lot heading towards London's house that was around the corner from the school.

CHAPTER 9:

MY DECISION

“Please come back to me NaNa,” EJ said as I began to get out the car. I turned towards him and kissed him. “If I were going to leave, I would have asked you to drop me off at Mike’s,” I said laughing. “OK, call me if you want me to come get you. Otherwise, I’ll come see you in your first class. I really do love you Kana” he said with sincere eyes. “I love you too.” I didn’t need to think about my response. I knew I loved him. I got out of the car and closed the door. He waited in the driveway until London opened the door for me. “What the fuck? Is that EJ, Kana? Why is he dropping you off? I heard you and Kai got into a fight today and I’ve been calling your phone for three days. Is it off?” London asked all these questions as soon as she opened the door before she would let me in. As I was trying to push through the door I said, “Hey London! I missed you too. Please let me in and I promise I'll tell you everything." She realized she was being a little aggressive so she gave me a hug. Then she stepped out the way so I could get in the door. I turned around and waved bye to EJ and blew him a kiss. I knew he wasn't going to do it back because he was too cool for that. When London closed the door she said, "I'm sorry Kana. My mom and I were so worried about you. Your mom called here hysterical, talking about some nigga named Eric had some guys come and get your things from Mike's house so you could move out to live with him. Now I see that Eric is EJ. I had no idea." "London, I've been through so much since my dad came and got me from your house. Let me speak to your mom and then let's go talk about it."" She isn't home from work yet but she's on her way. I'll text her and let her know you're here." She said, signaling for me to follow her to her room.

I took my shoes off and asked London to give me some lounge clothes. She handed me some basketball shorts and an

Aeropostale t- shirt (I know. But back then it was acceptable to wear outside and not only to sleep in). I sat on the bed and looked at my phone to see if EJ had texted me, although it had only been 20 minutes since I left him. I missed him. "Kanaaaaaaa!" London yelled dragging the syllables in my name out and anticipating the story I was about to tell her. "Okay I'm sorry. Where do I start? When we left your house, my dad told me he was enrolling me in school in Detroit and Kai was going to live with her biological mother." "Wait, she isn't your real sister and why did y'all have to do that?" London interrupted. "No she isn't but I'll explain that another time. Just listen. My mom cut Kai's phone off because I caught Kai and Mike in bed together, which is why I came to your house in the first place." London's eyes looked as though they were about to pop out of her head. She couldn't believe what I was telling her. Before I could finish the story, London's mom yelled upstairs "Girls! Come here please." "Fuck! It was getting so juicy. Please don't forget where you left off. I absolutely want to hear the rest of this." London said as she put her house shoes on and gave me a pair to put on. Little did she know, this story is damn near tattooed in my brain. I'll never forget it. When we walked out of London's room I saw my mom. I don't know how I forgot that my mom and Ms. Grant were friends. I should have known she would tell her I was over to their house. I was actually happy to see her, so many emotions filled my heart I began crying. (I bet you knew that was coming huh?) I ran to hug her. I'm so sure she had no idea what kind of mood I would be in. She started crying too and she hugged me so tight for what felt like an eternity. " NaNa we need to talk," Kim said. "Y'all go in London's room and we will wait for you in the kitchen. I'm about to prepare dinner," Ms. Grant said to my mom and me as she pointed towards London's room.

"Mom, I'm not..." before I could get my sentence out, she interrupted me. "Kana, I'm not here to make you come home. I understand why you left. I see so much of myself in you. I would have left too. I just hate that my decisions tore us apart and I hate that I drove you to that point. I know you tried to talk to me and tried to get us out of there but I didn’t listen. As a woman, you will make decisions that no one around you will understand. If you forget everything I tell you, remember this: When you make a decision, whether the decision is a good decision or a bad one, make sure you stand on it. Make sure you own it. I’ve decided to stay with Mike. Rather than make you stay with me, I accept your decision to leave and I won't fight you on it. I only ask that you don't shut me out. I ask that you learn from the mistakes you’ve watched me make and make better decisions. You’re my child so I know you can handle yourself out here. For some strange reason, I’m addicted to this man and I couldn't leave if I wanted to. I can't drag you down this dark path with me. I can only ask you to love me through it. Be there for me when I fall because I know I will fall. I pray God allows me to leave this relationship with my dignity. I promise you, when I get enough, I’ll leave. To be honest with you, I can't lose to Kai. If she is in fact pregnant by Mike, I have no idea what I'm going to do, but I'll cross that bridge once I get there." The fact that she admitted she was staying because she couldn't lose to Kai made me respect her so much more. In my opinion, it takes a strong woman to admit she is staying because she can't lose to another woman. "We won't tell your dad about this. We'll just tell him you and I moved back into the condo downtown. You have to continue to go see him like you always do to keep things normal. We will get through this together." My parents were married for 8 years. They married young, so my mom only really knew my dad. She didn't know what she was doing with Mike, but I could tell she had to find her way alone. She didn't want me to see her as less than the strong woman I knew she was. "Mom, Kai told me she was going to beat your ass because you decided to stay with Mike. I guess she was under the impression that they were starting a family together," I said to her as she wiped the tears from my eyes.

Laughing, she replied, “I’ll deal with Kai. You just keep her away from that man of yours.” I started laughing too. I pulled my phone out to call her from it. “He bought you a phone?” “Mom he bought me a phone, a few outfits, brand new pair of Jordan’s...” She interrupted me laughing. “I know. I saw them at the door. I can tell you lost your virginity. I hope you gave it to him and he didn’t take it.” With a stumped look plastered all over my face she could tell I needed her to elaborate. “Most girls will say; Oh yea, he took my virginity or I lost my virginity to him: not really understanding that there is a difference between someone taking or losing something and giving something. When someone takes or you lose your virginity, it wasn’t entirely up to you. When you give it, you made a decision to allow that person to be the closest to you that no one other than your child can be. You choose to let that person see you in your most vulnerable state. Basically when you give it, it’s your choice, you weren’t convinced. When you lose it, someone else made the choice for you or you made it unconsciously. Think about which one you did." "How did you know," I asked. Now readers, you know I was crying. "You're mine, I know you like I know the back of my hand. You've cried more during this conversation than you have your whole life," she said and we both started laughing.

In that moment, all I could think about was EJ and how I just wanted him to hold me. "Can you take me home please? I want to show you where we live," I said as I put on my clothes. "I thought you would never ask," she said as she stood up and hugged me.

CHAPTER 10:

S.W.P.H

“Can I come up?” my mom asked when we pulled up in front of the building where EJ and I lived. (I love the way that sounds) “I think I should share the convo you and I had with him and then we invite you over for dinner so we can all talk. I don't want to ambush him,” I said hesitantly because I didn’t know how she would take it. “I respect that. Don’t forget the plan with your dad and please don’t forget to call or at least text me every day” she said very calmly. I was shocked. I gave her a hug and kissed her on the cheek. “I won’t forget Ma. I love you so much.” Before I got inside the building she yelled, “I love you too Kana. Be careful and stay smart.” I felt so much better about living with EJ because my mom accepted it. I was so worried about what she was going to do. It felt like a weight had been lifted off my shoulders. I was on the elevator smiling.

I was just going over in my head how I was going to tell EJ about this exciting breakthrough in my life, well, really our lives. I came to the conclusion that I was just going to flat out tell him. There was no need to be dramatic. When I got off the elevator, I was immediately smacked in the face with the smell of weed. We lived in Unit # 708, not too far from the elevator. I turned the key and opened the door. I saw Swisher Sweets wrappers on the kitchen counter and two shot glasses. The house was very cloudy. I knew the smell in the hallway had to be coming from our house. There was nobody in the living room. I went to the bedroom and saw Kai on top of EJ swinging her hair. I screamed "EJ are you fucking serious!" EJ threw Kai off of him and took off running towards me. I ran in the bathroom and locked the door. I went through the bathroom into the closet to get the gun his dumb ass showed me how to use. I went around the opposite way back into the bedroom and aimed at the bed where Kai was rolling around laughing. I shot and hit the headboard of the bed. She screamed and ran out of the house with nothing but a bra on. EJ kicked the door down from the bathroom side and grabbed the gun from me. He threw me on the bed, climbed on top of me and said, "Kana, Baby let me explain!" His knees were holding my legs down and his hands were holding my arms down. I began crying and screaming uncontrollably, "You promised me no one would ever hurt me again. You promised me she was lying. You promised me I was safe with you!" He grabbed me, threw me over his shoulders and ran out of the house. The gunshot was loud so I'm sure the neighbors called the police. He ran into the garage and yelled, "Kana, I know you mad but we got to get out of here. Please don't try to run out of the car." I knew he was right so when he sat me in the front seat I didn't move. He did 100mph out of the garage according to the speedometer on the dashboard. EJ turned left to hop onto the expressway. "And to think, I just told my mother I loved you. She said she accepted that I was going to live with you. I asked you to tell me the truth. I gave you my all, in such a short time because you said I could trust you. You told me you wanted me to live with you because Mike was such a bad guy. You're the worst. You're a bad guy, acting like a good guy. At least Mike knows he ain't shit." As I was talking, I could feel the anger build up inside of me. Punching him was the only thing I could think to do. He started to swerve and yelled, "Kana would you fucking stop? You're going to kill us."

"I'm going to kill you. That's my goal, you fucking bitch ass nigga!" I said while I was still punching him and yes, crying. He could tell I wasn't going to stop so he got off the expressway and pulled over into a dark alley. He got out the front seat of the car to get in the back seat. "Come back here with me please," he said. "What the fuck are you talking about? No! What you need to do is buy me a ticket to Detroit! I'm getting the fuck away from all of y'all," I said as I turned around and folded my arms. Next thing I knew, he had me by my jacket, pulled me to the third row, and started to take my pants down. I kicked him in the face but that didn't stop him. EJ got my panties down and lifted my legs over my head. He put his tongue in between my thighs and I just lost all control and started crying again. “I am so sorry Kana,” he whispered as he stroked his tongue back and forth, up and down, around and around. I have no idea how he knew that would calm me down, but it absolutely did. He stayed down there for at least 30 minutes. When he came up he helped me get dressed then he kissed me on my forehead. He grabbed me, held me tight, rubbed my hair and whispered “I’m so sorry” over and over again. “Get in the front seat, I’m going to take you somewhere nice,” he said as hopped in the driver's seat and closed the door. I was at a loss for words so I said nothing and didn’t budge. He could tell I needed some time for my thoughts so he just started driving towards downtown Chicago.

When EJ and I first started talking, I told him a lot about me and my family. Something I talked to him about often was when I was a little girl, my mom and I use to stay at different hotels downtown. When we pulled up to one of my favorite hotels on East Superior Street, I knew he remembered me telling him that's where my mom and I went when one of us needed a pick me up. “I'll be right back Kana. Please don't leave” he said as he looked in the back seat where I still was trying to figure out how I let this piece of shit, get me out my panties again! I just couldn't believe that I just walked in on Kai again, but this time with my man.

I couldn't for the life of me understand why she wanted to hurt me. What did I ever do to her? I was always there for her! It was me and her against mom and dad. Whenever she did something bad, I never told on her. I was the best little sister a big sister could ever ask for. I told her I liked him so she knew how I felt about him. Before all this went down with her and Mike, she would hear EJ and me on the phone. She would ask me what I liked about him. She encouraged me to go with the flow and see how far I could go with an older boy. “All the seniors are going to hate on you because the whole school wants him. Look at my little sister, pulling older niggas," she would say in a proud voice. I just do not understand. More importantly, what did I do to EJ? I was minding my business. He came and begged me to trust him. He begged me to give him a chance. He was super persistent to the point where I was convinced that as long as he was around, nobody would ever hurt me. Not for a second did I think I had to worry about him as well.

"Ma'am, your boyfriend is asking that you come inside," the valet said interrupting my thoughts. I didn't have enough energy to tell the valet that he wasn't shit to me. I got out the car and walked into the hotel. EJ reached for my hand and I folded my arms so that he couldn't touch me. I followed him to the elevators and stood on the opposite side of the elevator. He pressed PH for penthouse. Every time my mom and I would come here, the PH was sold out. How the fuck did he pull this off. Being able to stay in the penthouse was one of my dreams. I was overly excited, I couldn't show him that though. The entire floor was the penthouse suite. He had to put the key in to press that floor. When the elevator stopped, there were roses everywhere. Chocolate covered strawberries and money spread out everywhere. There was at least ten thousand dollars as soon as I walked in the room. My eyes were lit up. I couldn't believe what I was seeing. "Did you know you were going to get caught? How did you pull this off, this fast?" I said snarling at him.

"Kana, baby sit down and let me explain," he said as he reached for my hand. I took his hand and he led me to the bedroom and sat me on the bed. I was super hesitant to sit down, but when I looked around and saw all the roses, I went ahead and sat down. On the bed there were twelve bouquets of pink roses, (my absolute favorite) and two white silk robes.

"I'm going to tell you the absolute truth Kana. Please don't leave me. I didn't tell you the truth before because I didn't think you could handle the truth," he said in a very shaky voice as if he was getting ready to cry. I blurted out "You didn't even give me the chance to see if I could. You just made that decision for me."

"You are right. I'm sorry. I promise from here on out I will tell you the absolute truth even if I think it's going to hurt you," he said as he kissed my hand. I was just so interested in knowing what happened that I just nodded and made a look that indicated it was OK for him to go ahead with the story. "I knew that Kai was staying with one of my homies, so I went over there to tell her to stop saying that we had sex. She was supposed to keep quiet because the first time was an accident. I came to her to ask her about you, and she came on to me. I told her that I really wanted to make things work with you and that I wanted to be with you and not her. She said she was going to tell you that she lied and she was just trying to piss you off. I thought that if I told you, I would lose you. I didn't know how you would handle it. After we talked and came to an agreement, I stayed and started smoking with my homie and she stayed. We started drinking

Patron and one thing lead to another and we ended up at the apartment. I thought you were staying at London's and I never thought you would catch me." While he's saying this, the tears were flowing down my face. Not because of what he said he did, but because I knew I was going to stay. I knew there was nothing he could do to me that would make me leave him. Everything about our situation made my heart skip several beats. The thrill of dating an older guy, the excitement of living with him, and the adventures he and I would go on and the things I would learn from him. With all those things considered, I couldn't allow this one incident to come between us. "Stop!" I yelled! "Just hold me and promise to never lie to me again," I said as he pulled me closer and held me all night.

Sometimes in life you come across a person that you know you would risk it all for, despite all odds, despite the looks, the negative comments. Sometimes, *Some Women Prefer Hell.*

UNTIL WE MEET AGAIN:

I wrote this book at a time when I needed a hero. I had to become my own. They say that if you write out everything that hurts you and burn it, that weight will be lifted off of your shoulders. Well, the shit that hurt me was too juicy to burn, so I turned it into a book. The events that took place in the book were life altering. We often feel that if we just keep the things that affect the way we live, think and breathe to ourselves, we will just get over them. From personal experience, that makes it worse. You could drink it away, but once you sober up, it's still ever so present. You could smoke it away, but when you come down off that high, it's still smacking you in the face. Just because you're in hell, doesn't mean you have to stay there but you have to fight like hell to get out of it. You have to make a conscious effort to put yourself and your feelings first, before theirs. Trust your gut feeling. It's there for a reason. We tend to over extend ourselves for the people we love, but doesn't that include (if not take precedence) when it comes to self? What if you took time getting to know yourself? What makes you happy, what makes you smile, what makes you sad, what makes you, you? Once you know the answers to those questions, you know your worth. When you know your worth, you teach people how to treat you. You do not accept less than you deserve. There is power in knowing who you are. We tend to settle for a familiar hurt than battle with the unknown of a new love due to fear of being alone or seeing that person with someone else. You block your blessings that way. I encourage you to press play on you. Take control of the outcome for your life. I promise you, no matter what you're going through, you are not alone. If you decide you want to stay in Hell to see the situation through, stay tuned for part two.

Love,

Modi

CPSIA information can be obtained
at www.ICGtesting.com
Printed in the USA
LVHW02s0453170718
583962LV00002B/11/P

9 780692 125359